Version 4.0. - Friday, October 28, 2022

written by

Denny Magic

Disclaimer

For all those wanna-be detectives out there... YES. I am well aware that whomever "Jack-the-Ripper" (From London England) really was, and the serial killer known as H.H. Holms (from Chicago, Illinois) are two very different individuals with absolutely zero connections to each other except for their heinous crimes.

Please keep in mind that this short story is a work of ***FICTION****.*

The various 'true facts' that I have used in order to enhance my story, only provided me with the basis of my tale, and should not imply that this entire story is based upon true facts.

Preface

I have always been interested in anything and everything that was ever written about *Jack-the-Ripper*. Primarily because the true identity of Jack has remained a mystery. *Jack-the-Ripper* remains an enigma, as the sands of time have all but erased anything that could be easily used to identify who he actually was.

All kinds of theories abound about who *'Jack-the-Ripper'* really was, and there have even been some speculation by wanna-be-detectives that he may have eventually sailed across the Atlantic to take up residency here in the United States to avoid prosecution.

It has been suggested by more than one wanna-be-amateur-detectives , that he changed his name and opened up a Hotel or Inn (a "House of Horror") where he may have continued his killing spree as a respectable property owner, providing rooms to young girls who were trying to secure employment with the Chicago World Expo.

All those theories remain completely untrue and nothing more than pure speculation, and there is no concrete evidence that would lead Scotland Yard, or U.S. Law Enforcement Services to conclude otherwise.

But if assumptions prevail by speculators who are sadly ill-informed... They would have us believe that the murders that were committed in London, and the subsequent murders that were committed in Chicago, were committed by the same person. That is undoubtedly 100% impossible.

My story is fiction, yes.

I have done my best to create some entertaining characters, and connections between some 'pie-in-the-sky' theories, and the few facts that are readily available.

Stringing what we do know, together with a bundle of "What If" scenarios in order to write a fictitious story... is what us creative writers do.

Despite the naysayers out there in the real world, I do hope that the rest of you enjoy my story for what it really is. Pure entertaining poppycock.

TABLE OF CONTENTS

London 1888

At 4:30 am the 'knocker-up' tapped lightly on the second-story bedroom window at the home of journalist George Lusk and his wife Collette.

George is a journalist working at the publication known as The Whitechapel Vigilance Committee a local London newspaper.

In an age where alarm clocks were yet to be widely used, having a person (the knocker-up) who would come-'round to tap on each person's window with a long pole, at a specific time of day, was the most reliable way to make sure that people were woken up so that they could end up going to work on time.

George had worked for the newspaper for almost four years. Mostly his tasks were rather mundane, and he was pleased just to have a job that lasted this long.

Collette his wife of ten years was always the first to rise after the 'knocker-up' made his rounds, and she hurried downstairs to make breakfast for George and their young daughter Minerva.

Collette always allowed George fifteen or twenty minutes extra time in bed, before she finally had to return upstairs to roust him out of the sack.

When she was successful... George, eventually shot out of bed like a bullet where he made his way into the restroom where he gave himself a quick once over with his straight razor. At least once a week he gave himself a bath too. George always seemed to be concerned about his hygiene and this was one thing that Collette found very appealing to her when they first met.

He was also quite the responsible husband when it came to being the breadwinner of the family. When she first met George , Collette's father tried to dissuade her from having any interest at all in a guy who just wanted to end up working for a newspaper. *"He'll never amount to anything young lady"* ...her father would constantly tell her, but Collette knew instinctively that George was 'the one', and she wouldn't entertain any thoughts of trying to find another.

They dated for almost two years, and after that her father finally capitulated. George's demeanor and personality finally worked its magic on her dad.

She wasn't aware of it at that time, but her mother liked George from the start, and as a result... her father didn't stand a chance of getting anyone in the family to turn their noses up regarding his daughter's love interest.

Even her younger sister (Mary) pined for George upon making his acquaintance.

Despite his interest, George's own family were not big fans of his decision to become a journalist either. His parents own a local butcher shop and his father had hoped that their only son would take over the business. But George had other ideas.

Despite George's decision, it wasn't too long before he became a little bored with all the low level assignments that were handed to him at the newspaper.

His duties at the publication seemed to usher in a plethora of mundane circumstances like a stolen bottles of milk from someone's front porch, or a lost pet.

The job provided a decent income, but... **EXCITEMENT** wasn't always forthcoming and he longed for a story with some 'meat in it'.

Then it happened.

Whitechapel 1888

Nigel Hathorne was the editor at the newspaper where George hung his hat. In the initial years that George worked there, most of the other journalists' who had been at the publication longer than he had, seemed to get all the "Juicy" stories.

He had studied long and hard in school in order to pursue this vocation, so he wasn't too anxious to 'throw in the towel' anytime soon, and he hoped that at some point that he would get a chance to pursue a decent story on his own.

He longed for a chance to prove to Nigel that he was a good... No... A **GREAT**... reporter.

Then one afternoon Nigel called him into his office. *"George. Please have a seat."* George took a seat in Nigel's office wondering if maybe he was going to get sacked. There was a long pause, as Nigel worked to clear paperwork off his desk first, before addressing George.

Then he said, *"George my boy, I called you into my office to see if you might be interested in taking on a new case?"* ...Nigel explained.

"Sir?" ...George answered.

"Last evening a young woman was found murdered in Whitechapel. A prostitute. I was wondering if you might have an interest in covering the story?"...Nigel explained.

George was silent as he considered the proposal.

Then Nigel chimed in, *"Before you answer, I must warn you that this is a murder case, and it's extremely grisly."* ...Nigel tried to explain.

"Grisly?"...George asked.

"Actually, it was quite horrendous."...Nigel shook his upper torso as he shuddered at the thought of the crime. Then he added, *"She was surgically disemboweled. It was quite a mess if I do say so myself."*

Then Nigel took a moment to size up George's reaction before adding, *"OK. OK. Maybe this is a bad idea."*

George immediately thought to himself that this might be his chance to gain some ground at the publication. *"No. No. I'm interested. Please. Go on."*

Nigel took a moment to try to get a read on George, then he added, *"Are you sure that you can handle something of this magnitude young man?"...*he paused.

Then he added, *"I mean, I would expect you to stick with this story all the way to the end. What I mean is. Once you sign on, you'd be expected to follow everything from a possible arrest all the way through a trial. Would you be willing to sign on for the duration of the entire case? That is, IF Scotland Yard is lucky enough to make an arrest?"*

*"Yes sir, I would."...*George answered, this time almost pleading.

Nigel sat back in his chair and smiled. *"Maybe we can finally get you off all those human interest stories, huh?"* ...He paused. Then he added, *"I assume that you'd appreciate that?"*

"Yes sir. That would be wonderful." George remarked.

Nigel privately wondered if he had made the right decision about approaching George. He realized that George was a young presumptuous fellow, but he held out high hopes for George.

Then he closed by saying, *"OK. George check in with dispatch so they can officially assign this story to you. You have my approval."*

George smiled, as he gathered up his thoughts before leaving Nigel's office.

He walked down the hallway, and then the circumstances suddenly hit him like a truck! He suddenly felt like he was on cloud nine. ***'Finally!'*** He had caught the break that he was waiting for. The opportunity that he had been working so hard for.

As he finally reached his work area, one of his coworkers, Sid Brown, approached, *"You still have a job pecker-head?"*

George smiled, *"Actually yes. I think I just got a promotion. Did you hear about that murder over in Whitehall last night?"...*George asked.

Sid smiled and then answered sarcastically, *"Yeah. Some whore had her throat cut and the killer cut off her titties too! Fucken pervert."*

George and Sid had been friends since George started working at the paper, but George realized early on that Sid could be a crass bastard, so he ignored his 'titty' comment.

Then Sid suggested, *"You want to get some fish & chips for break?" ...*George only smiled and nodded.

"OK. I'll come 'round later to pick you up." And Sid walked away.

George was a hard worker, and even he wondered from 'time to time' what he saw in continuing his friendship with Sid.

He knew that Sid was kind of a slacker, and even he occasionally wondered if hanging around with Sid might not be a bad decision. But he actually liked him despite all of his foibles. If nothing else, he could be very entertaining.

Sid fancied himself a 'ladies man', and George was often quite amused as he watched Sid try to connect with gorgeous women who were certainly out of his league.

He often thought to himself that if he was as homely as Sid that he'd NEVER approach a women of that caliber, and that's part of the reason why he always found Sid extremely entertaining.

He concluded that hanging around with Sid was kind of like hanging out with a comedian.

Regardless of his personal opinion of Sid, George was more interested in this new development, and he was anxious to tell his wife all about it, when he got home.

Passing on the Good News

When quitting time arrived, he was one of the first people to leave the building, and within minutes he found himself on the underground headed home.

The train station was only a half block from his walkup, and soon he was flamboyantly explaining to his wife what had happened at work.

Collette was noticeably pleased that this change might be viewed as a promotion of sorts. Even though it did <u>not</u> involve any mention of additional pay.

Yet... inside she was upset that all of this good news did come at the expense of 'that poor woman' who lost her life. But she rationalized that people all over London die every day, and it certainly wasn't her, or George's fault.

George was beside himself with excitement as he tried to recant the day's experiences to his wife, but Collette finally had to send their daughter to her room in light of the fact that George was beginning to discuss the murder in too much detail.

Once their daughter was sequestered in another room, even Collette cringed when George repeated Sid's comments that the murderer had cut off the victims breasts.

Immediately Collette asked George if he was going to be alright with such a high-profile murder case?

George answered, *"Well. I really don't know. I guess only time will tell, but every story at the newspaper wasn't going to be a tame little story about some juveniles who broke someone's window. Some of them might be about disgusting things that crazy people do. It's just part of the job."*

Collette tried to put on a happy face as she nodded in response to Georges analogy.

*"So, when are you officially going to start your investigation?"...*she asked.

George corrected her, "Coverage. The investigation part will be handled by 'the yard', and tomorrow I have an appointment with an inspector over there."

Then he added, *"But if I play my cards right, I will be the one to help pull the story together. The byline will be mine."...*George speculated out loud.

Scotland Yard

At seven am the following morning George showed up at Scotland Yard to meet with an Inspector. Detective Frederick Abberline.

He had spoken with the receptionist of the Inspector Division the previous day and supposedly Inspector Abberline had agreed to meet with someone from the newspaper. And George (at that moment) felt 'lucky enough' to be that person!

But right away George sensed that the constables' (which including Inspector Abberline) were not too overjoyed about the presence of any newspaper people.

The case was so new that there was a sense that the police were not too anxious to spill any of the facts to the general public through the press.

George immediately had a feeling that he wasn't exactly welcome.

Betty Perkins escorted George down the hallway to Inspector Abberline's office. As they entered she explained, *"This is that reporter fellow that I mentioned yesterday."*

George soke up first, as he held out his hand to shake. *"George Lusk."*

The Inspector completely ignored George's 'glad hand' gesture and remained seated and aloof, behind his oak desk without so much as a smile.

Obviously he was, 'all business'... and he didn't seem too interested in becoming George's friend.

"Yes. Yes. Well, eh. Take a seat Mr. Lusk." Then he finally looked up at George, flashing a very insincere smile. *"And what can I do for you, Mr. eh...Mr.?"*

But before George could introduce himself again, the inspector interrupted by saying, *"I hope this isn't* *going to take too long? I am a very busy man."...*He stated.

The receptionist was already in the process of busily leaving the room, but she had a moment to glance over at George and she tried to flash him an equally insincere smile. Somehow George sensed that she already knew that this meeting was going to be a challenge.

George became quite uncomfortable, as he sported a sheepish grin before he focused his attention back to the Inspector. *" My name is George Lusk, and I'm a reporter with The Whitechapel Vigilance Committee news."* ...He paused for a moment allowing that to sink in.

Then, not seeing any response...He continued. *"Well sir... Naturally my paper would like to cover that horrible murder that took place last night in Whitechapel?"*

The Detective sat there motionless for a long while, as he just sized up George, before saying a word. *"Yes. A most disgusting state of affairs to say the least."*

"I guess the first thing that I'd like to find out would be the victim's name?"...George asked.

"Hummmm. Well, we don't have a lot to go on at the moment."

He seemed to be evaluating George, then he continued. *"I guess I can tell you that. Now, we don't have any way to substantiate this at the moment, but from her personal belongings that were found at the scene... Her name appears to be Mary Ann Nichols."*...George sensed that Inspector Abberline was reluctant to even provide that little bit of information to him.

"So, you found her purse?"...George asked.

The Detective took quite a while to respond, then he said, *"Yes. Indeed."*

"We've heard that she was a prostitute. Is that true?" ...George asked.

With that Detective Abberline seemed to get a look of wonderment on his face. *"I don't know where you heard that, but that's what we're thinking, but please don't print anything about that until we can confirm it first. It's way too early in the investigation to make assumptions."*

"Do you happen to know how old she was?"...George asked.

"No. Not at this time, but she looked like she was in her early thirties, maybe thirty-four, thirty-five?" ...Inspector Abberline tried to answer. He seemed a bit annoyed.

"You know, we have always had a good relationship with the press, but you may be jumping the gun a little on this case. I mean, for God's sake, the murder is less than 24 hours old." ...Abberline argued.

"Yes sir. I can appreciate that. Look. I'm not here to make your job more difficult Inspector. I'm just trying to root out a few factual details so when the story

goes to press, all the facts are correct. I want whatever story that I do write to be accurate, that's all." ...George tried to emphasize.

He waited for a reply but didn't get one. So, he continued. *"A murder like this, here in London... is big news."* ...George added.

"I understand that Mr. Lusk, but in a case like this we don't want to expose everything that we know prematurely. If your paper reveals too much of what we know, it might hamper the investigation." ...He paused.

Then the Inspector added, "Look Mr. eh..."

George interceded. "Lusk. George Lusk."

The inspector continued, "Yes, eh... Mr. Lusk... I certainly don't want to impede your work, but please let us do our job ***first*** *before you start blabbing everything that I tell you in confidence in this office. I'm not attempting to be difficult, but I have a job to do as well."* ...The Inspector explained.

"OK. I understand. Believe me, writing a factual story is my one and only goal." ...George tried to explain so he could establish a 'working relationship' with the inspector.

Then George asked, *"We also heard that her throat was slashed, and if I understand things correctly, the murderer removed her breasts. Can you at the very least tell me if that's true?"*

"Mr. Lusk, I'm not sure who told you that but I hope to God that you're not planning to announce that?" ...Abberline emphasized.

George let his emotions enter the picture at that point, and he spoke out, *"Look, Detective. This story will NOT be released until I write it. Even if I tried to get it released as soon as possible, I'll still need to have some additional facts before I can write the damned thing. No offense."*

Abberline was silent as he stared at George, then he said, *"I think we're done here.."*

Then he craned his neck as he yelled down the hall to the receptionist, *"Betty... can you show our guest out please."*

The receptionist out front (Betty) got up and started walking down the length of the hallway towards Abberline's office.

But George was already frustrated, and he stood up, and held his hand in the air, *"Please don't bother, I'll show myself out if you please."*

He waved his hand over his shoulder as he vacated, and sarcastically added, *"Thank you for all your help Inspector."*

Back at the newspaper

George was steamed as he left Scotland Yard. Thank God that he had to wait for a carriage which allowed him to calm down a bit before he arrived at work.

As he passed Nigel's office, Nigel whistled and flagged him back inside before asking. *"So? How'd it go?"*

"Well. I seriously doubt that the inspector and me will ever become close friends, but at least he knows who I am." ...George tried to explain.

"Yes, well don't take things too personal. When I told Peterson that I was assigning this case to you I never saw him so pleased." ...Nigel explained, before laughing out loud. Then he added. *"He absolutely hates having to spend* ***ANY*** *time at all, over there with any of those stogy constables. Who did you meet with?" ...He asked.*

"Inspector Abberline?" ...answered George.

Nigel laughed. "Oh him? He's one of Peterson's favorites! A real bundle of personality he is."

He waited for a reply, and when he didn't get one he asked. *"So where do we stand?"*

"Well, he wasn't too forthcoming about anything. I suspect that it's a wee bit too early. He warned me to make sure that the paper didn't release any articles until Scotland Yard knows more."

"Did he give you any idea when that would happen?" ...Nigel asked.

"No. And I suspect that we could be, 'waiting until hell freezes over', if we have to depend on them notifying us about anything." ...George surmised.

Nigel laughed, before adding, *"Everything is difficult before it becomes easy my boy. In the meanwhile, why don't you go back to work on some of your other stories. But try to keep nudging this eh, Inspector Abberline. Remember, 'the squeaky wheel gets the grease'. Eventually something will break, that's how these things go."*

George politely excused himself as he moved towards his desk. Once he was seated in front of his typewriter, Sid burst in, unannounced.

"I had lunch today with Peterson. He was beside himself when he found out that Nigel assigned that murder to you. I guess he doesn't harbor any lost love for Scotland Yard. He hates that fucken place." ... Sid explained.

George could only smile and nod in agreement, then he chimed in. *"Well, I can't say that every constable is like the guy I met with, but he's definitely a wonker."* ...George sat back in his chair, then he asked. *"By the way... I was wondering... How did you know that the killer removed the victim's breasts?"*

Sid seemed to scan the office before explaining, *"A guy I know over at The Yard told me, I can't reveal who. But as you know when there's a murder in London, suddenly everyone has a theory, you know? Like the yanks always say, opinions are like hemorrhoids, sooner or later everyone has one."* ...Then Sid stood up laughing at his own joke, before leaving George's area.

The day's recap

That evening when George arrived home, his wife was absolutely giddy to discover what had taken place at Scotland Yard.

George was not only shocked that his soft spoken wife wanted to know all the details surrounding such a horrific murder, and the first thing that he did was send his daughter out of the room. *"Honey, why don't you give mommy and me a few minutes to talk, would you mind going into your room?"*

His daughter sighed, but finally made her way out of the kitchen. Once she was gone, George looked at Collette and smiled. *"Sometimes you really amaze me my love."*

"I hope that I always amaze you!" ...she added, with a big smile, as she leaned over and gave George a big kiss on the forehead before sitting back down in her chair. Then with conviction, she asked, *"So?"* And she waited for her husband's response.

George chuckled, *"It's a good thing that I'm not a constable but make no mistake... whatever I elect to pass along to you, cannot leave this house."*

Collette smiled, nodded, and brushed the air with her hand. ...Then George added. *"I mean it! Christ, the story hasn't even been printed yet, and the paper, and The Yard, don't want anything leaked to the general public. Everyone is worried that it might set off a state of panic. So, promise me?"*

Collette nodded... and she seemed to understand the seriousness of what her husband was about to convey.

That's when George meticulously related what had happened during his work day. In reality there really were very few <u>new</u> facts to relate, but Collette pressured him to reveal every detail that had taken place... Hanging on his every word.

As time marched on

A trickle of information leaked out from Inspector Abberline over the days that followed. But he always seemed to be holding back some information.

George was starting to wonder if his best connection might actually be Syd, before breaking out in laughter at that notion.

Mostly any new information came from the Inspector's Secretary which were called in by telephone to the newspaper's receptionist, who then had to relay written messages to the various reporters.

The only thing that was painfully true in 1888 was that although telephones were a brand-new invention to the business world in greater London... George was not privileged enough to have his own telephone, or even a number that was assigned to him.

So, he was forced to rely more and more on messages from the main receptionist that arrived for him from Scotland Yard through Nigel.

Why? Because his attempts to re-visit Inspector Abberline in person, were systematically stymied. It seemed that the Inspector had zero interest in seeing George a second time, in person.

Then "The Package" arrived and it somehow found its way to George's desk. It contained a letter supposedly written by an individual claiming to be the killer. AND... Half of a human kidney wrapped in butcher's paper.

George momentarily wondered if 'the letter' wasn't just a hoax. But when he unwrapped the kidney, it suddenly appeared that there was no doubt.

Plus, the killer mentioned in the letter, that he was including ½ of the victim's kidney... He also wrote that he was sending a second letter to Scotland Yard along with the other half of the kidney.

George did wonder if it wasn't just a cow's kidney, while growing up in his family's butcher shop, he had seen a lot of meat-biproducts in his life, but... if it was indeed a hoax, it was a damned convincing one.

But George didn't want his own 'reluctance to believe', to hamper his progress with the case. If everything was legitimate, it was the break that he was waiting for. So, he immediately pushed that completely out of his mind.

Quickly he made his way down the hall to Nigel's office. Together they collectively concluded that the package was indeed real. Disgusting, but real, none-the-less.

Because the killer made a reference to sending a duplicate package to Scotland Yard, he asked Nigel to place a call on his phone to Inspector Abberline's office.

Once the connection was established, Nigel handed the telephone to George who took a seat in Nigel's office.

"Inspector Abberline?" ...He asked.

Duplicate deliveries

Inspector Abberline answered, *"Inspector Abberline here."*

"Good afternoon Inspector. I don't know if you remember me? This is George Lusk. The reporter from The Whitechapel Vigilance Committee newspaper.*"*

There was a pregnant pause and then the Inspector said, *"Yes. I remember you alright. What can I do for you Mr. Lusk?"*

"This morning the paper received a package from some person claiming to be the killer of Mary Ann Nichols." ...George explained.

"Uh huh?" ...muttered the Inspector. He almost sounded uninterested. *"O-Kaaaay?"*

George wanted a different response from the Inspector instead of what seemed to be indifference... but then he realized that maybe the Inspector hadn't seen the duplicate package yet.

When he didn't get the response that he was hoping for... he added. *"Along with the letter was half of a human kidney."*

There was an inordinate silence, and then quite suddenly... Inspector Abberline surprised him by asking, *"Are you available to visit my office this afternoon?"*

George replied, *"Absolutely. I can be there by two o'clock if that's OK?"*

Inspector Abberline confirmed the appointment and George hung up.

Nigel was noticeably excited, *"What'd he say?"*

"I have an appointment at two o'clock this afternoon." George explained.

A huge smile began to spread across Nigel's face, and he immediately leaned over and playfully punched George's shoulder, with a sense of confidence. *"Good work my boy."*

Finally, a break

When George arrived at Scotland Yard, he made his way towards the receptionist's desk where Betty was sitting, but before he could engage her in conversation, she waved him down the hallway and pointed vigorously towards Inspector Abberline's office.

George made his way down to Abberline's office and immediately the inspector pointed at a chair, indicating that George should take a seat.

Then in a rather commanding voice he told George how things are going to proceed. *"OK Mr. Lusk, apparently this particular killer wants as much attention as he can get. But if we're going to be working together, I want to make sure that we're on the same page. The department does not want some rogue reporter spilling the beans prematurely with every potential bit of information, and I hope that you understand this?"* ...Inspector Abberline laid out the rules quite clearly.

"Yes sir. The paper and me realize this, and we hope that you will eventually view us as an asset, and NOT a hinderance." ...George explained.

Abberline was silent as he stared at George, still sizing him up. Then he opened up. "Alright then. Here's what we know. The victim was indeed a prostitute, and yes the killer was absolutely brutal. He literally removed her breasts, and her vagina as well. We think that he had already slit her throat, so we suspect that she was already deceased before he defiled her further. At least everyone here hopes that she didn't suffer. We suspect that he's either a medical student, or... maybe even a doctor who may have a medical practice here in London... I say that because he used something like a surgeon's scalpel on her... the cuts were so precise, anyway that's how we see things. There was a lot of blood at the scene, and apparently he made sure that he performed this dastardly deed in a dark alley well away from prying eyes... as all of this obviously took quite a bit of time. Unfortunately there were no witnesses at the crime scene.

He paused, "Although... A carriage driver said that a very well dressed gentlemen approached him around ten pm and wanted to hire him to take him 'round St. James Park." ...Abberline related.

"10 PM? Aren't carriage rides over by at least 7 or 8 PM?" ...George asked.

"Yes. You're right about that, but this driver had a few very late customers, and by the time this fellow approached him, he was already finished dressing down his horse and was ready to call it a night." ...Abberline explained.

He paused, then added. *"But he said that the guy offered to pay him double if he'd return to service, and he agreed."*

"Did he say where he dropped this fellow off?" ...George asked.

"We should be so lucky, huh? No such luck. He said the guy got out at the same spot that he picked him up at." ... Abberline explained.

"Did he leave any personal items in the carriage?" ...George asked.

"No. Nothing. But the driver did offer a detailed description of the guy. And before we continue, keep in mind that this is **ONLY** a lead... This fellow could be entirely innocent and unrelated to the crime."

He paused before continuing, "But, the driver was sure that he was an aristocrat of some sort, and not some commoner. He said that he was dressed as if he may have attended the theatre earlier that night... a theatrical play or some other sit down event, maybe even the Opera? We're trying to check all the theatre houses that had performances that evening. The driver said that he apparently was dressed like someone of importance, right down to the black leather gloves.

The driver noticed that because it really wasn't a cold night, he thought that the gloves were just an accouterment that he used to enhance his appearance. He was also carrying a cane, but the driver said that he didn't seem to need a cane in order to walk. But when he saw how this fellow was attired, he figured him for a decent tipper 'after the ride', and he was right. He said that this fellow gave him a guinea after paying his fare, and he was glad that he was still able to take him around."

"Well." George took a deep breath and slumped in his chair as he processed everything that Inspector Abberline had already related. Then he asked, *"It's too bad that there weren't some additional clues or something that you could work with?"*

"Well, " ...and Abberline went silent as he stared off in the distance for a brief moment.

Georges curiosity went wild and he leaned forward, *"Well, what?"*

"The driver did mention that although it was dark at that time of the night, he thought that he spotted a fairly large stain on the guys white shirt. He said that in the back of his mind, he speculated that it might be a blood stain. But it was dark, and he was unable to conform that."

George smiled. And he thought to himself... 'Now we're getting somewhere'. But investigating the murder was the constable's job and not his.

However, George finally felt that the relationship seemed to be moving in the right direction between him and Abberline. At least now, he had some facts to work with, as he tried to piece together the whole scenario.

Then Abberline interrupted, *"I suspect that you're very anxious to publish something in the paper?"*

"Yes sir I am." ...George answered.

"OK. Here's what we're prepared to authorize. If you'll agree to just stick to the basic facts... that a murder was committed in Whitehall and the victim's name, then we're prepared to authorize the story. But no mention about the disfigurement of her body, or anything that I just told you about this little jaunt in St. James Park... and ABSOLUTELY NOTHING about that blood stain." ...Abberline demanded.

George asked, "Can I offer some details about the victim? Like her address, and eh... the fact that she was a prostitute? I mean, I need something that my editor will consider some real meat to my story."

Abberline stared at George for a moment then added, *"I think that would be permissible. But I want you to run everything by me before it hits the newspaper. If you receive anything else, at your end, from this lunatic, I want you to telephone me before you print anything. Will you promise to do that?"*

George smiled and nodded, then he added, *"But I don't have a telephone. I can call you from Nigel's office if anything else arrives from this nut case."*

Inspector Abberline held up a single digit and picked up the telephone on his desk. He dialed, and George heard him say, "Yes, get me over to Nigel at The Whitechapel Vigilance Committee." He waited...

"Hi Nigel. Good, Good, Look I have your reporter here in my office... George?... Yes. Yes. Look... I have a small favor to ask. George and I are going to have to remain in close contact throughout this murder investigation, and I was wondering if you might consider installing a telephone in his office?"

There was a long pause.

"OK. Great I was hoping that you'd say that. Oh yes. Yes, she's doing much better now. Yes. Me too. Thanks, my friend." ...and the inspector hung up the receiver.

As Abberline hung up he felt the need to explain... *"My daughter's been very sick. But she's doing much better now."*

George smiled and said. *"I have a daughter too."*

Abberline did not comment but only took a moment to smile at George. Then he stood up and held out a hand to shake, adding, *"I hope we can start over Mr. Lusk?"*

George smiled back and stood up to shake. Then he said, *"Yes. We already have. And please call me George."*

His own Telephone

Within the week a brand new telephone arrived and was installed into George's work area. Immediately Syd was jealous and started hanging around near George trying to make use of the phone, but once Nigel saw this he came over to set things right.

"What in the hell are you doing here Syd, don't you have something to do?" ...Nigel demanded.

"Well, eh, yes sir." ...Syd sheepishly announced.

"Then get to it, and under no circumstances are you to use George's telephone. UNDERSTAND? I mean it Syd. If I catch you... you'll be looking for another job. Understand?" ...Nigel explained.

"Yes sir." ...Syd replied.

Nigel was reaching the end his rope with regards to Syd, and he left George's area angry.

"Geezus Christ, what the fuck is wrong with that guy" ...Syd asked as if the problem was with Nigel.

"Look Syd, I consider you a friend, but you need to straighten out before you lose your job." ...George chimed in.

"Yeah, I guess you're right. I really need to keep this job or the old lady will boot my ass out." ...Syd explained. And Syd left George's area with his tail between his legs.

As time went on, George's running commentary in the newspaper drove the public to become increasingly more aware of what had transpired.

It wasn't only George's commentary, but the very real fear that a lunatic killer was roaming the streets of London. George wasn't exactly sure when it happened...but it wasn't too long before the public started calling the killer... 'Jack the Ripper'.

As Inspector Abberline speculated, it was mainly because of the extraordinarily brutal nature of the murders as George's coverage of the crimes was allowed to expand. Over time George was allowed to include more and more details about the first murder in his newspaper story.

Then it happened again in Spitalfields. And it wasn't too long before killings were taking place every six or seven months.

First Annie Chapman, then Elizabeth Stride, followed by Catherine Eddowes, and Mary Jane Kelly became the latest victims that happened over a period that lasted several years.

They became known as the "canonical five".

The prominent connection between them all was that the victims were all prostitutes.

By that time... Inspector Abberline and George Lusk had become very close friends.

The legend grows

Soon extensive newspaper coverage bestowed widespread and enduring international notoriety on the Ripper, and the legend solidified.

A police investigation into the series of eleven brutal murders committed in Whitechapel and Spitalfields between 31 August and 9 November 1888 are often considered the most likely to be linked to 'Jack the Ripper'.

However, clues were as scarce as 'hen's teeth' and Scotland Yard was unable to connect all the killings conclusively.

The killer was not only brutal, but he was extremely intelligent, and he left the constables scratching their heads. They were clueless.

The murders were never solved, and the legends surrounding these crimes became a combination of historical research, and folklore that captured the public's imagination.

When everything was said and done... the conclusions were mostly speculation about who and why this lunatic committed any of them. Then as quickly as they started... they stopped.

Once the situation calmed down in London, things finally began to return to normal.

However, the legend of 'Jack the Ripper' endures.

The RMS OLYMPIC

The sister ship of the Titanic was the RMS Olympic and this day in 1898 is sat fully loaded with provisions and a gluttony of anxious passengers.

As passengers made their way up the gangplank to board the luxury liner. A tall rather debonaire gentleman took a spot at the railing looking down at the crowd below on the main pier.

A band played popular music of the day, as part of the 'departure celebration' for this luxury liner, on its way to New York City.

A beautiful young woman in her early thirties moved closer to this fellow who was standing at the railing and she accidentally bumped into him. *"Oh, I'm so sorry sir, please forgive my clumsiness."* ...She explained.

The man smiled. *"Please, please don't worry. No harm done."*

There was a somewhat uncomfortable silent moment between them, and then she smiled and asked... *"I take it your going to New York?"*

The man chuckled before answering, *"I'd venture to say that the answer has to be a resounding 'YES'. I suspect that everyone onboard is going there as well."* And he laughed.

The woman realizing her faux paux covered her mouth and shook her head, *"Yes, yes, of course. That was an ignorant comment, I apologize. I hope you'll forgive me?"* Then she held out her hand and said, *"I'm Gertrude Kutcher I'm from Liverpool."*

The man reached out and shook her outstretched hand, *"I'm Hubert Horace Holmes, but most people just call me 'Dr. H'."*

"Ah ha. That's quite an unusual moniker... H." ...she commented. And then she smiled.

The man asked, "I guess that probably does sound a mite bit humorous as well."

"No, no. I was just thinking to myself that most of the people that I grew up with, called me Gerty. I hated that. But what are you gonna do huh?" ...she explained.

There was a somewhat uncomfortable silence, then she asked, *"If I can be so bold, are you and your family traveling to America on vacation?"*

Holmes laughed. *"No, I'm the proverbial bachelor. I'm traveling all by myself. I liquidated my medical practice in London and I hope to reestablish a new practice in Chicago, Illinois. How about you?"*

"Chicago? I'm headed there myself. You know they're looking for people to work at the Exposition, and I hope to secure a secretary position with their business office." ...she explained.

"Well, it's nice that your family is willing to relocate to Chicago to support your dreams." ...Holmes replied.

"No, no. It's not what you think. They've come to the conclusion that I'm crazy. No. I'm traveling all by myself, I hate Liverpool. If it were up to me mum and dad I'd be working in the family's business making

shoes. I know how to do it, in fact I've become quite a cobbler... but, I've had it with that life. Smelly feet and all! I want to live in a big city, to be surrounded by all the music, and the action... you know?"

Just then the ship's fog horn blew which was quite loud, so the two of them gave up their conversation trading it for a brief pause.

After the noise subsided Holmes spoke up first, *"I guess were about to set sail?"* Gertrude smiled and nodded.

A moment or two later, a loud notification whistle blew followed by an announcement that came over the public address system, *"Eh Ladies and eh Gentlemen, This is eh Captain Formingaza speaking. Please eh have eh you tickets handy and eh be sure to connect with one of the pursers that will be coming around to meet with you on the main deck. They'll take eh you to your assigned rooms, and eh... Welcome aboard the RMS Olympic."*

Holmes smiled at Gertrude and he asked, "I hope that you will not think it rude of me, but I'm on the upper deck, in room 516... I hope that you might allow me to share a meal with you in the coming days?"

Gertrude smiled. "Why yes Dr. H I would love that. But I have to warn you I am just one deck above the crew quarters below. In the dungeon no less. I'm traveling on a budget, so nothing fancy for me." ...There was a pregnant pause.

Then she added, *"Here, Let me give you my room number."* And she dug out a pencil and a scrap of paper from her purse, where she wrote down his room number first, and then her own, before tearing the scrape of paper in half and giving him the half with her room number on it.

Then she said, "I*f you don't think I'm being to forward... I'm in a very small inside room. Number 310. And yes. I'd love to have dinner with you once we get settled in."*

"Wonderful. If I may, Why don't I give you a call this evening?...Holmes asked.

"I'd like that, but there's just one problem." And Holmes waited for an explanation.

She tried to explain sheepishly, *"I don't have a telephone in room 310. How about this... when they announce dinner in the main dining room, what say we meet up again – in the dining room?* "

Holmes smiled. Just then a purser approached the two of them, *"Good afternoon. My, my, what a handsome couple."*

Gertrude immediately corrected this fellow, *"No, no. We just met. We're traveling independently."...* And she glanced up at Dr. H and smiled.

He purser seemed a bit embarrassed but managed to plough forward, *"My apologies, well... miracles do happen on these trips, one never knows."* ... and he took both of their tickets.

After inspecting the two tickets he announced. *"Looks like room 310 and room 516 right? OK... If the gentleman won't mind waiting I'll escort this young lady to her room first? Then it will just take me a few minutes and I'll come back to get you sir. If you'll remain right here I can be back in a moment or two."*

Dr. H smiled and nodded.

Dinner for two

As the doctor unpacked his clothes... the onboard public address system came on with the notification that 'Dinner would be served in the main dining room precisely at six pm. Dress would be 'formal this evening.'

Dr. H took a quick glance at his pocket watch and felt comfortable that he could enjoy a cocktail on his balcony before getting dressed for dinner.

His mind was kept busy as he pondered his meeting with Gertrude.

Gertrude's room was NOT outfitted with a speaker, but a fellow who was staying down the hall, took it upon himself to knock on several doors to pass on the message about dinner.

She was excited and right away drew a bath in order to get ready. She had been thinking about her meeting with Dr. H - all afternoon. He had really left quite an impression on her.

After making herself presentable, she hurried up to the main dining room and a maitre'd approached.

He spoke up, *"Are you dining alone this evening Mame? And if so, would you mind if I sat you at a table with some other guests?"*

Right away she answered, *"I'll be dinning with another fellow traveler, so if you don't mind, can I request that you locate us at a table by ourselves?"*

He smiled and took a 360 degree gaze around the dining room before catching the attention of a waiter. Then he held up two fingers and the waiter nodded as he pointed at a nearby table. *"Alright... you see that fellow over there? He'll seat you Madam. Bon Appetite."*

She entered the massive dining room, as the maitre'd turned to assist other new diners.

She made her way over to the waiter who pulled out a chair and helped her get situated. She was pleased about the location because she had a direct line of sight to the main entrance so she could watch for Dr. H to arrive.

Ten or fifteen minutes later, in walked Dr. H, and right away Gertrude stood up and began waving to get his attention.

He spotted her and smiled, excusing himself from the maitre'd by pointing towards her. The maitre'd... after putting 'two & two' together smiled and stepped aside.

Gertrude sat back down and was absolutely giddy that Dr. H had finally arrived. Right away through an almost uncontrollable smile she greeted the doctor. *"Good evening Dr. H. I wasn't sure if you'd show up."*

"Yes, yes, and a good evening to you as well Ms Gertrude. As you can deduce, I am a man of my word, and I happen to be hungry." The doctor took a moment to scoot his chair in, then he scanned the huge dining room just taking everything in. *"You know, this is the first cruise ship that I have ever been on, and I must say it is quite opulent isn't it."*

Gertrude laughed, "Well the entire ship doesn't look this nice; I can assure you. Unless my room is the exception? My cabin is like an overgrown closet. No windows, no view, and if you don't mind me speaking out loud, extremely claustrophobic." She paused before continuing, *"At least when the lights are out, and I climb into that overpriced tiny little bed, it doesn't matter."*

The doctor tried to smile but did his best to act sympathetic, *"Gertrude, I'm so, so, sorry to hear that. I couldn't stand to be confined like that. I don't want to seem forward, but before we arrive in New York I hope that you'll consider allowing me to show off the suite that they put me in? I think you'd love it."*

There was a long pause while Gertrude stared at the good doctor intently, and smiled coyly. *"Yes. I think that I'd like that."*

Just then the waiter arrived with two menus, he handed one to each of them. Then he announced, "Tonight we have three main entrees available. The first is a broiled half pound lobster tail, or a half-inch slice of prime rib which is available in rare, medium, or well, and lastly a one-inch rib eye steak... also available in rare, medium, or well. Each comes with either a baked potato, or a generous portion of Garlic Mashed Potatoes, or a generous serving of fresh garden peas, or broccoli."

At that moment another one of the kitchen's hired help brought a basket of sliced French Bread and some whipped butter on two small dishes with two little butter knifes.

The waiter stepped out of the way for a brief moment while this other fellow positioned the bread and butter at the two place settings.

Then the waiter resumed his spiel. *"We'll get you started with either a fresh garden salad, or a bowl of the chef's special Boston Clam Chowder. It an American recipe! So, what can I get for you folks?"*

Gertrude was giddy, and said, *"Well, I'd like a salad, AND a bowl of chowder, if that's permissible?"*

"Yes Mame absolutely, in fact if you order one of the main entrees and then you decided that you want a second serving... it would be my pleasure." ...the waiter explained.

Then he continued... "Ok, a bowl of chowder and a green salad for the lady, and what kind of dressing Mame?"

"Do you have 1,000 Island?" Gertrude asked.

"Yes Mame. And Gertrude nodded. Then he looked at Dt. H. *"And for you sir?"*

Dr. H spoke up, *"I'll have the salad with Italian or Balsamic dressing... No beets or olives please."*

The waiter added, *"Which dressing would you prefer sir? We have both of those."*

Dr. H answered, *"Balsamic would be my preference."*

"Then *Balsamic it is*. OK then, which entrée would the lady like?"

"Hummmm, I'm not too sure that I can eat such a large portion."

And the waiter interrupted, *"Don't worry. We can wrap anything that your unable to finish, and you can take it back to your room. That's not a problem Mame. People do that every day."*

Gertrude smiled and said, "Oh that would be lovely, thank you. Well... I think I'll have the lobster then; it'll be the first time I've ever eaten that. All my life I've been told that I should try it someday, so..."

The waited replied, *"Lobster. Alright, and would you like the Garlic Mashed potatoes or a Baked Potato?"*

"Baked please." ...Gertrude answered.

"And Garden Peas or the Broccoli?" ...he asked.

"I'll have the garden peas." ...Gertrude answered.

"OK. And for you sir?" ...he asked the good doctor.

Dr. H smiled and replied, *"I think I'm going to have the Prime Rib, medium please... with a Baked Potato and the Broccoli."*

"OK. I'll keep an eye on you both to see how you're doing with the salads before I have your entrees brought out. Are you good with water or would you like to order a glass, or bottle, of wine?"

Immediately Dr. H spoke up... *"Yes can you bring us a bottle of your best dinner wine... French if you have any?"*

"Yes sir, if I may be so bold, I would recommend, Chateau Cos d'Estounel it has a nice nutty flavor that is not overwhelming. Would you like two glasses or a bottle?" ...the waiter asked.

Dr. H was quick to respond, *"Go ahead and bring us a bottle and a couple of new glasses."*

Then the waiter smiled and added, *"I'm required to mention that a wine of that caliber would be considered an optional purchase. Is that alright with you sir?"*

Dr. H smiled and added, "Yes, yes. That's perfectly fine. I'm in room 516."

The waiter made a quick note and smiled, then he nodded, "Coming right up. And thank you for choosing to sail with the RMS Olympic.

Gertrude was beside herself with bewilderment, because she noticed that the waiter did NOT write a single thing down before leaving with their orders. "Amazing."

"What's amazing?" ... Dr. H asked.

"That guy must have a wonderful memory? He didn't write any of this down." ...she volunteered.

"When you were working in your parents shoe shop did you write everything down that the customers told you?" ...the doctor asked.

"Are you kidding? My father expected EVERYTHING to be written down. That was required." ...and she shook her head.

Dr. H spoke up, "Well, I suspect that our waiter has been performing this job for so long that he has the entire menu for each and every day memorized.

"Uncanny to say the least." ...Gertrude acknowledged.

Then she added, *"By the way, I've only had a sip of wine once before in my life."* Then she made a face and shook her head in disgust. *"I hated it! I thought it was disgusting."*

D. H laughed, *"Well, I suspect that you're going to love this wine. A good wine of this caliber would be hard to match any place in the world. I'm not tryin to say that the wine that you were introduced to was of poor quality... but... If you decided that you don't like this one, then you are definitely not a wine connoisseur."*

Just as the doctor finished explaining, a new lady arrived with the wine and two brand-new wine glasses. She carefully uncorked the bottle and filled Gertrude's glass about half way, then she poured a quarter inch into Dr. H's glass and he picked it up, swirling the wine around in a circle and sniffing the glass before he sat it back down on the table. The server waited for this inspection ceremony to take place and after he nodded with a smile, she filled his glass and sat the bottle down on the table. Within a second or two she was gone.

Gertrude spoke up, *"My, my, do you have to do that with every new bottle of wine that is ordered on a ship like this?"*

Dr H laughed, *"No. But in a fine restaurant, or... on a ship like this, when you order such an expensive bottle of wine it's sort of expected to go through that ceremony."* They shared a laugh over this.

Then she raised her glass and took a small sip, "Ummmm, that is good. I like it." ...Then she asked, *"I hope you won't think it rude of me, but can I ask how much this stuff costs?"*

"I'm going to guess that it will be around 30 to 40 pounds. But please just try to enjoy it, and don't worry about the cost." ...the good doctor emphasized.

As the dinner moved forward Dr. H asked a lot of questions about her, and Gertrude asked an equal amount of questions about him. His practice in London, and his education. Gertrude, being a lot younger than Dr. H, didn't have as much of a past to reveal, but they made good use of their time together to educate themselves about each other. This transpired over the course of the evening.

Gertrude finally looked around the restaurant and realized that almost all of the guests had left for the night.

Kitchen help were busy vacuuming the carpet and just cleaning up in general. However, as a courtesy no one bothered her or the doctor.

"It looks like we're gonna be responsible for closing the joint." Trying to be humorous she added, *"I guess if we stay long enough we can end up eating breakfast together."* ...Gertrude said.

The doctor smiled and reached across the table to give her outstretched hand a gentle squeeze. Then he spoke, *"I'd like to have breakfast with you Gertrude. That is if you'd allow that to happen?"*

It was a somewhat awkward moment, but Gertrude smiled, and looked down. Then she looked at Dr. H and smiled, *"Maybe you can show me your fancy suite?"*

Dr. H smiled back and gave her hand a squeeze. *"Good, come on let me show you how the other half lives."*

The Doctor's Digs

The two of them took a long slow walk all the way to room 516. Dr. H retrieved his key and unlocked the door to his suite. He reached in turning on the electric light switch and stepped aside so Gertrude could enter first.

"My God. This place is enormous, what is it two rooms?" ...She wondered.

"Well, if you count this living room there's actually three rooms. The living room and two separate bedrooms, a master and a guest room. Don't look in the guest room I just threw all of my junk in there and it's a mess." ...He explained.

"Will you get a load of that bathroom. Holy cow! My bathroom has a tub and a loo with a sink right above the toilet. You can't even lean back, you have to sit there all scrunched up, it's that tiny." ...she was bowled over.

Then she walked over and opened the French Door that led out to a huge balcony, as she stepped outside she took in a huge breathe of fresh air at the railing and with the full moon reflecting on the ocean she was mesmerized. Then she said, *"No wonder you seem to be such a happy fellow... I could stay her for the rest of my life."* Not hearing anything back from the doctor she turned only to discover him standing right behind her, before she could resist he reached around her waist and pulled her closer, and he kissed her on the lips.

She seemed to resist at first, then she relaxed and actually embraced him back. They stood there kissing for at least a half hour. Under the moonlight the ocean was as smooth as glass with a rather warm breeze wafting across the balcony.

She felt like she might be dreaming, but she knew that she wasn't... and she was happy. Very happy.

Hours later in the dead of night Gertrude whispered into the doctor's ear... *"Can we have breakfast together?"*

"I have an order sheet for breakfast sitting on that desk over there. All we need to do is mark what we'd like to eat, and room service will bring it at the designated time." ...Dr. H explained.

"Room Service?" and she shoved him playfully... *"Get out! Are you serious?"*

"Yes. I'm serious. All we need to do is fill out what we would like to eat, and the ship's staff will prepare it

for us, and bring it right to the room at the designated hour." ...He explained.

"Do you have to telephone it in?" ...she asked.

"No. No. Once you fill it out there's a clip on the outside of the door, and as long as you put it outside before 6 am, the purser will pick it up and see that it finds its way to the kitchen. We tell them what we'd like, and when we'd like it delivered, and Voila! It's supposed to work like magic." ...Dr. H explained.

"But you've never actually tried using this service, right?" ...she asked.

"Well, actually no. Like you... This is also my first cruise. But when I was escorted to my suite the purser explained how this works. Why don't we get a little bit adventurous and give it a try. Besides, I'm not letting you outta my sight. I'd like you to stay." ...Gertrude smiled playfully, and slid under the covers, soon she was soon performing fellatio on the good doctor.

A the morning sun was filtering in through the balcony doors, the two were awaken by a gentle tap on the door.

Dr. H got up out of bed and could see that it was already light outside, and he figured out that it must be the designated time that the two of them wrote on their breakfast order. So, he slipped on a robe and answered the door. A young waiter was standing there with a food cart... he glanced at the order and said, *"Dr. Holmes?"*

"Yes." Replied the doctor.

"I have your breakfast order." He explained.

"Oh yes. Good. Good. Please come in." ...Dr. H acknowledged.

The waiter pushed the cart into the suite, past the surprised doctor, and over to a fairly large round wooden table, where he began to move all the breakfast plates and accouterments onto the table where he arranged them for two people.

All this while Gertrude continued to remain asleep.

Then he rolled the empty cart a little ways back towards the door and he stood up, *"Will there be anything else sir?"*

But when Holmes said 'no' he didn't leave. That's when Holmes realized that he was waiting for something. Then he realized that it was a tip.

Holmes touched himself on the forehead and smacked his lips together realizing that he had to get to his trousers which were still 'balled up' at the foot of the bed, he comically fumbled with them searching for his wallet, and some English Pounds, and when he found some cash he looked at the fellow and asked... "Will English Pounds be alright?"

The guy smiled and said, *"Yes sir that would be very generous of you."*

Holmes handed the guy some money and soon the waiter was only a brief memory.

Gertrude actually did returned to her confined room, where she played the role of a single traveler to maintain the image with the few travelers that were also sequestered, on the same level (floor) as she was..

In the late 1800's a young single woman needed to maintain some sense of dignity... at least publicly speaking.

Young women needed to try to prevent others from thinking that they were promiscuous. Gertrude was raised under these assumed rules and regulations, and even though her tryst with the good doctor were repeated night after night... she was guilt ridden and did her best to keep it a secret.

But, as exciting as being on the ship was... having the doctor's penis in her was even more exciting and she was enjoying it beyond words.

Therefore, during the daylight hours she'd use the tub in her room, change clothes, and make sure the purser and anyone else that was in the immediate area could see her coming and going in and about her room. Then each evening she spent rendezvoused with Dr. H.

Her ignorance about the fundamental of a potential pregnancy were thrown out the window. She thought... 'He's a doctor. If he isn't using any protection, he must know something that I don't know and then she concluded that he probably cares for her a great deal. She had convinced herself that he would

NOT risk getting her pregnant if he didn't care for her. She was convinced that he wouldn't do that.

Two days from New York City

Gertrude accompanied Dr. H back to his room that evening after dinner, which had by now become a nightly routine.

It was a beautiful evening with a light breeze rolling across the ocean on a moonless inky black night.

Gertrude was busy enjoying the sea from her vantage point at the railing on the Balcony.

Everything was wonderful as she was finishing up a cocktail that the Doctor had fixed for her, when suddenly she felt his hand lift her dress.

Then he gently nudged her upper torso so that she leaned over the railing, as he exposed her backside before pulling down her panties to expose her bare ass.

Then he fondled her rear end, before sticking a finger first in his mouth, and then gently in her rectum.

After a few minutes, he took a cushion from one of the lounge chairs and got down on his knees and began licking her ass with his tongue.

He used his hands to nudge her legs apart further and further spreading her ass cheeks.

It was then that he slid his hands slowly down her legs until he reached her ankles, where he firmly grabbed a hold of them.

Suddenly without warning, he lifted her right over the railing and she went overboard.

He stood up and smelled her ass on his hands before laughing out loud.

He went back into the room closing the balcony door, and after positioning himself on the bed he began to masturbate.

The inquiry

No one had any idea what had happened to Gertrude Kushner, the Captain launched an inquiry and they did spend some time asking Dr. H some questions becdause some of the hired help had mentioned that they weremspendinga lot of time together... but the final consensus was that she must have fallen overboard.

A day later the ship pulled into New York and the whole matter was lost in a pile of red tape and legal ramblings. Holmes knew that Gertrude's absence would be a case that would eventually just fell through the cracks.

He had gotten away with yet another murder. People that met him later all thought that he was just a happy go-lucky fellow, but they were wrong. Killing brought him great joy in life. It made him smile.

He was addicted to the heinous acts that he had committed, going back to his time in London. And he used that friendly demeanor like a mask to hide his real self.

At the New York Dock he paid a carriage driver to take his belongings and him to the train station where he boarded a train for Chicago.

Buying real estate

When Holmes arrived in Chicago he started to research what was available in an area that was close to the fairgrounds. He had remembered what Gertrude Kutcher had told him about all the young girls that we heading there to try to get jobs at the world's fair.

With an appetite for young women... that's where he wanted to relocate to. Instead of him having to roam the darkness of the night searching for his next victim, and risking getting caught... he'd try to setup some close by building where they would come to him.

He decided that he could purchase some sort of commercial building and renovate things turning it into a kind of hotel, or inn.

He could offer inexpensive rooms to young women, making the rents so affordable that it would become known 'through word of mouth' as a place where a young woman could afford to live while they tried to secure employment at the expo.

Holmes had quite a financial nest egg and he was therefore able to seek help from Commercial Real Estate developers.

After all, he was a Doctor which he used to persuade real estate sales people into trusting that he could afford such a purchase.

He had a satchel full of large denominations of English Pounds... By today's standards he was traveling with slightly more than two million in US currency. That was an enormous amount of money back then.

But that did not present any problems for commercial real estate people who were eager to sell him whatever it was that he was looking for.. They knew that English currency was easily exchanged for US Dollars. And once he showed them his bank statement, they were willing to do backflips to get his business.

He had become acquainted with a real estate salesman by the name of Clyde Jeffries. He actually liked this fellow, and Clyde showed him three commercial buildings... he final came up with a foreclosure that was 'priced to sell, and fast.

Dr. H eventually paid Clyde a check for ten thousand dollars as a deposit, and it wasn't long before his offer was accepted.

It was a corner building that was once the home of a small manufacturing company and had sat empty for a number of years.

The building in Chicago that eventually became the "Holme's Murder Hotel"

Holmes envisioned that he could pay to have the upper two floors converted into a sort of Hotel (or Inn) and he figured that he could subdivide the ground floor into several independent store fronts that he could rent out.

When Holmes took possession of the building it was sorely in need of basic upkeep. He took this to be a good omen, because he wanted to covert the upper floors into a place that looked very inviting to prospective female borders, but it woulkd hide secret passageways, two-way mirrors and a litany of dastardly features all designed to encourage his murderous ways.

It would include an elaborate basement that would provide a private space where he could 'dispose of dead bodies' without being interrupted.

He had a special spiral stairway installed that ran all the way up to his private quarters, so he could come & go at will, without being seen.

It also had a sort of 'laundry chute' where he could dump the remains of the women that he intending to murder, and then send their limp corpses sliding all the way down into the basement, unseen by prying eyes.

Holmes made purchases of medical equipment, and he acquired several kinds of caustic acids and deadly gasses that he planned to incorporate into his dark deeds.

Some of the rooms were outfitted with gas lines where he could trap unsuspecting women in their room's and then gas them to death while they slept.

He also had a great desire to practice necrophilia, and was anxious to 'get started'... so his first priority was to design the layout and then he would delibertly hire building contractors from areas outside greater Chicago to come into the city to work on bits and pieces of the project until it was done.

By compartmentalizing these projects, he could avoid any contractors from seeing the Big Picture.

They didn't know one another, so he was fairly certain that they would not be getting together to share information about what was taking place.

There are a lot of drawings and depictions that are on file for the general public in various archives, and what follows are some examples.

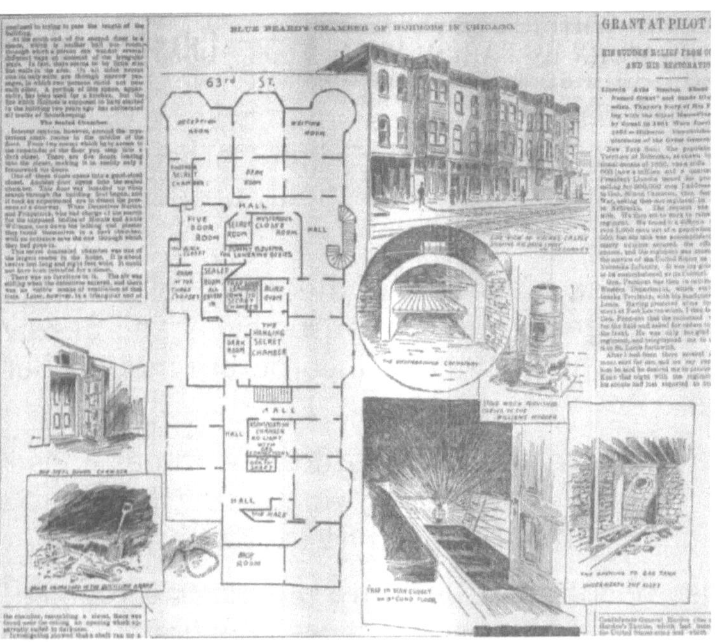

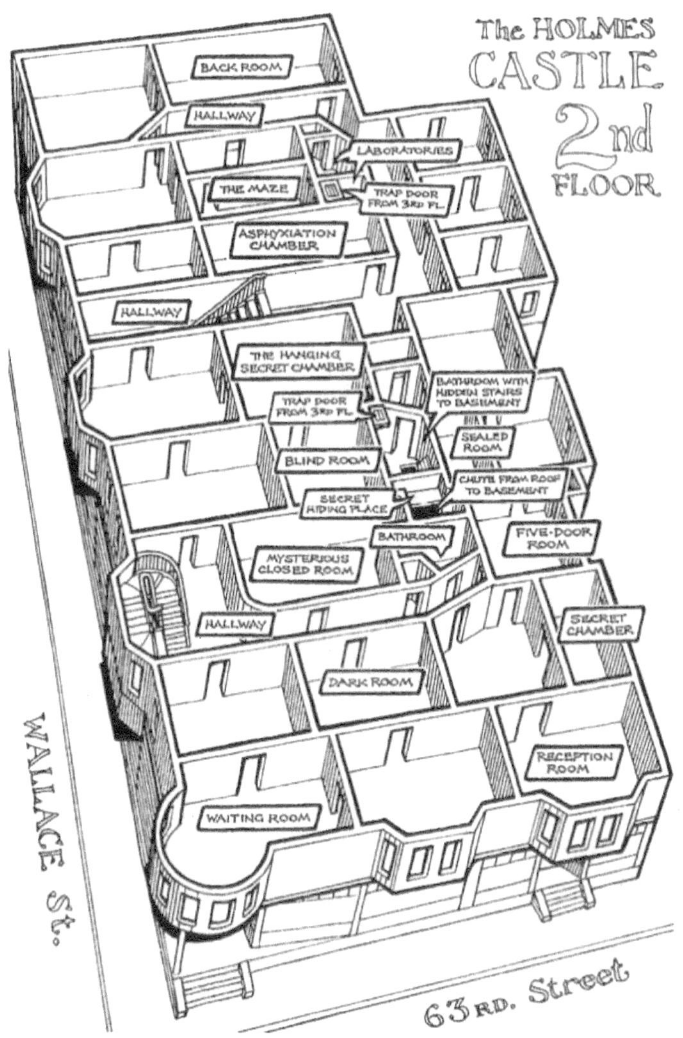

It took almost a full year before the "Murder Hotel" was completed, but Holmes was meticulous and very articulate about building a murder machine.

And when it was completed he took a look in a mirror and smiled. All the store fronts were rented out meticulously so that the products that were sold there had a strong appeal to young women. Everything was done to draw in young, beautiful, women.

When Holmes opened for business he didn't have to wait long for his first victim to arrive. She made her way up the stairs to the second floor registration desk and rang the bell.

Holmes was a bit unprepared and immediately grabbed a coat, so he would looked presentable as he made his way out to greet her.

Holmes smiled, *"Yes. Can I help you?"*

"Yes, hello. My name's Sharon Crawford, and I was told that I might be able to rent a room here, but it sort of looks like you may not be open yet?" ...the young woman explained.

"Well, it's funny that you would notice, but yes. We're a brand new hotel and we just opened for business... yesterday in fact. I apologize for all that new wood smell, but the carpenters just finished up everything. In fact, we haven't even had a chance to have the new housekeepers sweep up all the saw dust yet. They'll be here tomorrow. I apologize." ...Holmes explained.

Sharon smiled, "Oh ok. But I guess my question is can I take a look at your room rates, and if we can agree could I be your first customer?

Immediately Holmes smiled (thinking to himself – victim number one) and then he added. *"Why of course!"* and he turned the brand new registration book around, and then fumbled under the counter for a fountain pen and some ink which he relocated to the desktop. *"You know, we're so new that I haven't even been able to post our room rates yet, but here's the sign."* And he held up an 18" x 20" sign that displayed all of the room rates.

"Oh my?" Sharon exclaimed.

"Oh, I hope you don't find us too expensive?" ...Holmes said.

"No. No. I guess I was just shocked to see how reasonable your room rates are. No. You're quite affordable, I guess the rumors that I had been told were correct. But can you show me around before I pick a room?" ...Sharon asked.

"Of course, of course. Because you're going to possibly become our first guest, since the renovations were completed, you can have your choice of any room that you'd like! How often have you heard that before?" ...Holmes smiled.

Sharon smiled and let out a robust laugh at this fellows sense of humor, *"I have to say... NEVER! But I'd be honored."*

There was a moment when she looked deeply into Holmes eyes and they shared a smile together. He seemed like a very nice fellow.

Soon Holmes was walking her through the hotel showing her one room after another. And by the time they returned to the registration desk she was convinced that the rooms were immaculate and of course brand new construction. And that this place was indeed a 'steal'.

Holmes led her back down to the main entrance and asked her to sign the registration book. When she was finished he turned it around and said, *"Sharon Crawford from Racine, Wisconsin huh? What brings you to Chicago Ms Crawford?"*

"Well, I'm a steno and I take shorthand, so I was encouraged to come to Chicago to see if I could get work at the main office with the World's Fair. The Expo? I was told that getting work her would be fairly easy, and I need a job, so... Here I am." ...Sharon explained.

As he listened, he filled out her 'room card'. Copying all her contact information over from the registration book. He would start keeping a card for each guest in a small wooden box. Of course, Sharon's was the only card in the box at the moment.

"Are you planning to rent rooms to families as well?" ...she asked.

"Oh no. My policy will restrict the guests to young men and young women who, like you, are seeking work at the fairgrounds. No kids, or pets. We want to gain a reputation as a nice safe and quite place, where people such as yourself can relax after a hard day at work.

Sharon was encouraged by this news.

When they were done Holmes grabbed the room key and handed it over to her. Then she reached down to pick up her travel luggage, and he stopped her. "Please, please I'll get that for you." And he came around her side of the counter and picked up her bag.

As they made their way towards her room, she jokingly asked, *"Where's your bell boy?"*

Holmes laughed and he smirked at her playfully, *"Your looking at him!"* and he laughed along with her. *"Maybe someday, but right now I'm not only the desk clerk, but the bell boy as well."*

Once they reached her room, and he put her bag on a luggage rack, that's when she asked, *"Is there an inexpensive place to eat around here?"*

"Yes, several! Because we're situated very close to the Fairgrounds... we're surrounded by fairly good places to eat. But later, after you've been hired by the Expo... and I am certain that you will. I understand that you'll get an employee's discount that can be used at all the food vendors on site. Those discounts will be difficult to match at any of the regular restaurants located around here. Until then, Pedro's is a great little Mexican Restaurant just down the block. There's also an Italian place within walking distance. " ...He explained.

Then Holmes left her room making his way back to his personal apartment.

He was beside himself with glee, and when Sharon returned from dinner, he immediately made his way into the secret hallway that ran across the rear of several of the guest rooms.

Each had peep holes built into the soundproof wall that gave him access to each room through a two-way mirror that was attached to the wall in each room.

When Sharon returned from dinner, he made his way into the secret hallway adjacent to her room immediately, and he pulled up a stool so he could get comfortable to spy on her.

He watched as she took her clothes off, carefully putting her garments into the dresser until she was completely naked.

He liked what he was seeing...

Then she actually walked up to the mirror, completely naked and he watched as she handled her breasts as if she was posing for a nude picture.

She lifted them and at one point she began to suck her own nipples first one than the other.

Then she began to ungulate from side to side, as she seemed to be inspecting her lovely body. He liked that she had stiff long nipples, then she made her way over to the bed and he was pleased to see that she began to masturbate.

'My God', he thought to himself. This was an unexpected pleasure, so he dropped his trousers, pulled down his boxes, spit in his hand, and began to masturbate along with her.

When she started to cum he could see her withering on the bed, but because the wall was soundproof he was unable to hear her enjoy her orgasm.

It was obvious that she was really enjoying herself, that's when he shot sperm all over the wall. Yes. He was going enjoy killing this one.

cattle for the slaughter

Sharon did secure employment with the World's Fair Office, and she paid Holmes for a full month. By the end of the second week two additional women rented rooms... Sally Karnac, and Louise Mitchell.

Two young men also came by to rent rooms, but Holmes told them that the place was all booked up just so he could get rid of them.

Holmes had a routine by that time, after dinner he'd make the rounds.

Sally was apparently a nymphomaniac, and she masturbated every night on cue, but he found that Sharon only pleasured herself every few days.

Louise was apparently very religious and before climbing into bed each night she spent a lot of time on her knees praying silently for what seemed like an hour.

He was privy to seeing all of them naked at one time or another, and he soon lost interest in Louise as she was not sexy and had small insignificant breasts that reminded him of a teenager.

But he did find that her teenaged appearance eventually did turn him on, and he finally gave in to his urges.

One evening he opened the gas valve flooding Louise's room with a gas that was used during medical procedures.

Once he knew that she was unconscious, he evacuated the air in her room by way an exhaust system, then he entered though a false wall, and he took off her night shirt and sodomized her.

Afterwards he tried to insert his penis into her mouth, but she was completely unconscious and after failing at this, he carried her body inside the secret passageway and over to the chute that was set to a forty-five degree angle that led all the way down into the basement. He dumped her body and watched as she slid effortlessly down into a laundry basket in the basement.

Then he made his way down a secret stairway and once he was there, he dismembered Louise's body, and cremated her in the oven.

The exhaust ran through a pipe on the outside wall of the building, all the way up the side, more than 15 feet above the roofline where it vented to the sky.

No one would recognized the smell, because the neighborhood's air [in this part of Chicago] was filled with all kinds of odors.

He thought to himself, 'only a mortician would potentially recognize that particular smell anyway, and the nearest funeral home was miles away'.

It took more than an hour to dismember Louise's body, before he could put the body parts into the oven for cremation.

As he was finishing up, he wondered if Sharon might be masturbating tonight. He glanced at his pocket watch and wondered if he'd have time to catch her in the act.

Once Louise was safely in the oven, he started the cremation process. Then he made his way back up to see if Sharon would be putting on a show. And as luck would have it, she was in the throughs of orgasm when he started watching her.

Once she was finished, he gassed her, and once he was sure that she was unconscious... he entered her room through a false wall, and tried to rape her, but he was unable to get a second erection and finally gave up trying. All he could do, after fingering her vagina, was to smell his fingers.

Besides, he knew that he'd have to get serious about covering his tracks regarding the murder of Louise Mitchell.

If anyone came around looking for Louise he'd have to concoct some believable story in case anyone started asking too many questions.

So, he called it a night and went to his private quarters.

Besides, he knew that he'd have to completely clean Louise's room the following day and that could take a while.

It would require a full cleaning, that would involve getting rid of her clothing and personal possessions.

The following morning, he ran into Sharon who was headed off to work. *"Have you seen Louise by any chance? I tapped on her door but she didn't answer."* ...Sharon asked.

"No. As a matter of fact, early this morning she left me a note on the registration desk that explained that a family emergency had come up and she was headed back home. I was just headed up to her room to figure out what I needed to clean so the room is ready for my next guest." ...Holmes explained.

"Oh, I'm surprised. I thought that we were becoming good friends. I guess I'm just a little surprised that she left without saying goodbye? That's all." ...Sharon shared.

"She didn't share any home address information in the registration book... Did she give you an address for her family? I mean perhaps you could write her a letter?" ...Holmes explained.

Sharon was deep in thought... "No. She seemed like a woman who valued her privacy. We didn't spend too much time together, but I really liked her. Oh well? Ok, it is what it is..." Then she smiled at Holmes and added, "I have to get to work. Take care Mr. Holmes."

Holmes smiled and said silently to himself... 'I'll take it anyway that I can get it you little bitch!'

No end in sight

Over the next few years there was a never-ending-stream of young unattached females that kept the building filled up.

Holmes made the rounds drugging them and having arbitrary sex with all of them at one time or another.

Some he murdered, and some he didn't.

Holmes lost interest in any women who were homely or didn't keep their hygiene up to snuff. Ironically most of those 'unkempt tramps' actually lived to 'tell about their experiences'. They had no idea that their looks or their bathing habits actually saved their lives.

Once Holmes got a whiff of a smelly vagina, or... if they were borderline ugly... he lost interest in them sexually, and many just moved out a day or two BEFORE he actually killed them. So, in essence, their poor hygiene actually ended up saving their lives.

There were several other situations that caused him to take 'pause' with regards to his murderous habits.

Once a family from Missouri made the trek all the way to Chicago looking for their missing daughter. Because she was last seen at Holmes's Murder Hotel, the father made a beeline to see Holmes.

Holmes had no idea, but this guy's daughter shared some suspicions in a letter that she had sent home, and when she disappeared... The father put 'two & two' together, and being a suspicious fellow he dragged the entire family to Chicago to 'see for himself'.

The father was a retired Chief of Police and he smelled a rat, when he evaluated that letter, explaining what a creep that his daughter thought that Holmes was.

He was suspicious and wanted to investigate Holmes for himself.

Fortunately for Holmes, he had become an expert at cleaning up everything after a murder so that even a well-schooled investigator would have had quite a task to find even one clue. However, Holmes was becoming over-confident, and that almost became a challenge whenever he wondered if he'd actually get caught. He always concluded that he was way smarter than any policemen.

A partner?

Over the next two years word of mouth helped keep the Murder Hotel at full occupancy.

On several occasions men continued to try to book rooms, and usually Holmes was able to dissuade them. But, once in a while he could not avoid renting rooms to a few of them.

When he did notice that a particular male resident was a homosexual and had male guests. He just evicted them. The few that resisted... he killed them.

Homosexuals (at that time) were looked down upon by people in general... and Holmes knew that NO ONE would come looking for a pervert like that, and they didn't.

Then one day a fellow in his early thirties showed up looking to rent a room. He was an odd little chap.

His name was Martin Waxmeir. Holmes noticed right away that Martin was a little bit weird. He worked at a printing company just three blocks down 63rd Street.

The first thing Holmes noticed about Martin was during his initial interview, as he was attempting to dissuade Martin from becoming a renter... by casually mentioning that most of the people living there 'We're Women' and that he, 'probably wouldn't be too happy living amongst a bunch of women'.

Martin's eyes lit up and he smiled, with an oddball wink of his eye, *"Oh no, your wrong about that..."* ...and he subtilty grabbed the crotch of his pants giving his penis a squeeze and trusting his pelvis into the air like he was having sex. "I'd like a chance to meet a lovely young woman. Nothing would please me more than getting some strange ass! I bet you've had a tryst or two with some of them?"

Martin's antics and comments actually appealed to Holmes. He may have found a potential 'partner in crime'. That's when he scratched his chin, and added, *"Say, IF I agree to rent you a room, would you be interested in doing a trade for a partial discount on your rent?"*

"Hummmm. What's the catch?" ...Martin asked.

"Well. I could use some help around the place, minor things like helping me keep the place clean, maybe cleaning a room or two once in a while, after a guest moves out. Things like that." ...Holmes tried to explain diplomatically.

"That sounds great, but you do realize that I already have a full time job at Fischer's Printing Shop down the street? Yes?" ... Martin tried to explain.

"Yes. I saw that on your registration, but what I would ask is that you ONLY consider this as a spare time job. What I mean is... IF you have some free time, then from time to time... maybe you'd consider doing a little bit around here to help me out. I'm trying to run things all by myself, and because we're usually at full, or nearly full occupancy, I'm finding out that it's hard for one guy to handle this place all by myself. I suspect that when you wanted to help out, that would probably be enough, and I would then be able to credit you. I'd just take it off your rent. What do you think?" ...Holmes explained.

Martin took a moment to consider Holmes's offer. He walked over to the window and looked out, as if he was thinking thinks over.

Holmes finally asked, *"Well? What do you say? Do we have a deal?"*

Martin walked back closer to the registration desk, before answering *"And if I end up getting lucky by fucking one of the tramps that live here, you wouldn't mind?"*

Homes smiled, *"As long as I wasn't fucking her myself."*

Martin smiled and held out a hand to shake, "DEAL!"

Holmes put Martin in the room next to his own.

It was only the second room in the entire building that wasn't outfitted with two-way mirrors, hidden doors, or any of the gas inlets that Holmes had been successfully using to control the female guests.

Being an opportunist, he realized that this Martin fellow would not be hanging out all day because he'd be at work, and then in the early evening hours, or... on weekends... maybe he'd be able to help Holmes lighten his own work load. That would free him up to go back to his perverted lifestyle. He missed that.

For the first few months things returned to normal.

Holmes would molest a new girl for a few weeks, and then ultimately some of them would confide in him that 'somehow' they had become pregnant, which all of them volunteered was... "IMPOSSIBLE"... seeing as they were either a virgin or had not been with a man for years. They could not understand how this could have happened.

Inside Holmes would be laughing himself silly, knowing full well that HE was the father.

The problem was that those particular women had received their prognosis from a doctor's office.

He knew that any Doctor worth his or her salt would be following up on the condition of his or her patient. He realized that he couldn't have that. So, one by one, he did away of those girls, ASAP.

Then after Martin had been living there for more than two years, one day he accosted Holmes in the office.

Holmes immediately surmised that whatever it was that Marin wanted to discuss was business related, *"Yes Martin what's on your mind?"* ...He asked.

Martin seemed a bit exasperated as he slumped down in one of the chairs in front of Holmes's desk. Well, you know that I've been fucking that Julie woman in room 8?"

"Yes. How's that going?" ...Holmes asked.

Martin flagged him off with his outstretched hand... *"Good. Good. But now she tells me that she's pregnant!"* He paused for a brief moment. *"I mean, I have no intentions of marrying that bitch."*

There was a long silence that filled the room, then Holmes finally spoke up, *"Well. I may have a solution for you."*

Martin smiled and asked, *"An abortion?"*

Holmes smiled and said, *"More of a permanent solution than that."*

Martin leaned forward to hear what Holmes had to say, "Yeah?"

Holmes fidgeted in his seat for a moment, and then he asked, *"Can you be trusted to keep a secret?"*

Martin sat up straight and smiled, *"Goddamn right I can. I was trained as a spy in the military."*

"OK then. I want to show you something, follow me." ...explained Holmes. And he stood up flagging Martin with his outstretched hand. "But you have to promise me that you'll keep your goddamn mouth shut! Follow me."

Holmes made his way to a secret stairway that led down into the basement. He stopped briefly, turning towards Martin, *"What I am about to share with you cannot leave this building, right?"*

Martin didn't have a clue about what Holmes was going to show him, but he instinctually realized that it was something serious. And he nodded.

Holmes backed up his statement by saying, *"I'm not fucking around here Martin, if you ever tell anyone about this it could cost both of us our lives. Comprende'?"*

Martin nodded.

Then Holmes looked down and added, *"OK. Then follow me, and watch your step."*

The two of them made their way down the narrow steps.

Showing off the basement

When Holmes turned on the electric lights Martin let out an audible gasp. *"What the fuck is this? It looks like an operating room at some hospital."*

Holmes smiled and laughed, *"Well in a manner of speaking it is. This is where I'll help you get rid of your problem?"*

Martin took a step backwards wondering 'what problem', and Holmes picked up on his body English right away by explaining, *"The pregnancy?"*

Martin took another look around the room and asked, *"You do abortions in here?"*

Holmes began to laugh, *"No. No. Dissections. OK. I can see you're a little bit confused. Here have a seat and I will try to explain."* Holmes dragged over two chairs and both of them sat down.

Holmes began to unravel what had been taking place since he was known under another name, way back in London. Jack the Ripper.

No distain

Instead of disgust Martin seemed to hang onto every word that came out of Holmes mouth, and he seemed to take delight in hearing about the mutilations that were performed by Holmes on his earliest victims, going all the way back to the time that Holmes lived in London and was referred to as 'Jack the Ripper'.

As Holmes described some of his earliest deeds, Martin would let out a small chuckle. He seemed to be impressed with Holmes, especially after hearing all the sordid details of each and every murder.

Martin's casual response, which was devoid of any signs of disgust, help to persuade Holmes that he might be someone that could be trusted. So, he did not hold back anything. The more Martin seemed to be interested, the more he wanted to share with him.

Besides, if he decided that Martin couldn't be trusted, he could have murdered him on the spot, and cremated his body that very afternoon.

He was quite surprised that Martin's demeanor never changed throughout the entire guided tour of the autopsy room in the basement.

He thought for sure that when he showed Martin the cremation oven, that he might protest in some way, and he was ready to murder Martin right away if that happened.

But... Martin treated the entire presentation by Holmes as a sort of invitation to join in. This titillated Holmes almost as much as any of the murders he had committed in his lifetime.

Murder is a serious business, and it took a while for Holmes to become totally confident that Martin could be trusted, but... he had an inner feeling that he was willing to take a chance on this fellow. He surmised that they might be cut from the same cloth.

Besides, he had realized that another set of hands would help him cycle through the victims more efficiently, and faster. He harbored an inert desire to step up the killings. Having new victims cycle through the Murder Hotel was titillating to him. Just the thought of that happening, almost made him cum in his shorts.

Martin didn't ask too many questions. But the questions that he did ask... mostly revolved around the murder process.

Enticing the victims to rent rooms at the "Murder Hotel" was something else that Martin seemed to be interested in, and... the ways that Holmes screened through applicants, so that when they disappeared... Local Police and/or relatives didn't come snooping around asking a lot of questions about their disappearance.

When there was a break in Holmes presentation, Martin spoke up enthusiastically. *"As long as I have a chance to fuck some of these cunt's, I'm in!"*

Holmes smiled and reached out a hand so the two men could shake on it.

"OK. Let's not get ahead of ourselves, but just let me say this... IF I ain't fucking a particular woman myself, then yes! You can do whatever you want with the others." ...Holmes explained.

Martin immediately asked in an excited tone of voice, *"And if I find myself bored with a particular woman that I've been fucking? Or some sort of problem arises?"*

"You just let me know, and together we'll put that potential problem to rest." ...Holmes spoke.

There was a long pause as Martin mulled over the arrangement. Holmes watched as a big smile spread across Martin's face.

Then Holmes added, *"You know many of these bitches have some valuables and some even have a large chunk of cash when they come here. I'm also willing to cut you in with a third of whatever we find, just to insure that you'll keep your mouth shut."*

Martin smiled and laughed, *"Shit I would have been happy just to be able to get so much ass on a regular basis. But yeah, if you're willing to do that too... it would be a bonus, but I can assure you that I know how to keep my mouth shut."*

Holmes smiled. He finally realized that he had a 'partner in crime', *"Good! But I need to ask... You ever kill anyone?"*

Martin smiled, "I killed a bunch of Germans in the war.

Then he added enthusiastically, "So, Yeah... you can count on me to kill any of these bitches without any remorse."

Then he paused and added, *"Fuck, just say the word and I'll murder anyone that you point at."*

"That's what I wanted to hear! OK." ...Holmes smiled as he shook his hand.

The years that followed

Over the next four years between Martin and Holmes they racked up nearly 60 additional victims. That allowed Holmes to claim nearly 50 of them for himself, when he counted the women that he murdered in London.

The debauchery was horrendous, and the two men we're despicable beyond belief.

Every horrific sexual deed imaginable was tried and accomplished by at least one of them.

Often they encouraged the other fellow who actually did the deed. Sometimes Holmes would watch Martin fuck one of the girls, from the safety of the hidden hallways through the two-way mirrors.

And sometimes Martin would watch Holmes. There was no regret, or remorse.

Cameras had started to become popular with members of the general public, and because the

Murder Hotel was situated close to the World's Fair, hundreds of thousands of people were snapping photos like crazy in the fairgrounds and in the surrounding neighborhood.

Holmes was worried, and never allowed his photo to be taken by anyone, let alone a guest.

Martin wasn't as careful.

Holmes tried to explain that 'if one of those photographs that were hanging in the basement, were to reach a missing victim's family, that it could link their disappearance to the 'Murder Hotel' and intimately to Holmes.

However, soon Martin talked Holmes into buying a decent camera, and keeping it in the basement, he also set up a small darkroom where he taught himself how to produce pictures of the woman's dead bodies.

Those included women holding Martin's penis in their mouth, their hand, their vaginas, and even in their rectums.

This he tried to do well before their bodies were dismembered and cremated.

Surprisingly, Holmes was not only worried about having these photos plastered all over the basement walls, but ironically he had very little interest in taking similar photos of himself and the women that **he** murdered.

Martin seemed to value the photographs almost like some sort of trophy.

Holmes approached Martin on several occasions, reminding him that the photographs had to remain in the basement.

Only after Martin agreed did Holmes allow Martin to play around with his newfound interest in photography.

Initially when Martin was finally assisting Holmes in the autopsy room, and with the cremation process... Martin suddenly wanted to start saving severed breasts from his victims, but Holmes was very adamant and didn't want to leave anything around for the authorities to find. So, he said, "NO."

As a result, Martin gave up the idea of collecting severed titties, but he did continue to collect photographs of his victims in all kinds of compromising positions.

Everything was fine until one day... Martin stopped in at the local grocery/liquor store. He had become a regular customer and was on a first name basis with the store's owner... Jeffery.

On that particular day after grabbing a few items in the store, he sat his groceries down on the counter, and he pointed at a particular brand of whiskey and asked Jeffery to add that to his bill.

Then he reached into his back pocket and as he reentered the store he tossed his leather billfold onto Jefferies counter.

Then he made his way back into the store to gather up some additional groceries. The store was empty of other patrons. So, he left his wallet on the counter.

Jeffery picked up the wallet as he walked deeper into the store, trying to get Martin's attention. "Eh you left your wallet my friend!"

And as Martin was walking away he yelled back, "Yeah, I need to get a few more items, there's a ten spot in my wallet... Go ahead and take that out to cover everything."

Jeffrey nodded, and opened Martin's wallet he spotted a picture in there that clearly showed a naked woman sitting in a chair with Martin's erect penis in her mouth.

He could not take his eyes off of the photograph.

By that time Martin had returned to the checkout counter, and he literally grabbed his wallet away from Jeffery. He fished out the ten spot that he had mentioned and handed it over to Jeffery for payment.

"Is that even legal?" ...Jeffery asked?

"Look my friend, the less you know the better. OK?" ...Martin said with a sense of anger.

"I was just curious, that's all." ...Jeffery asked.

"LEGAL?" Martin seemed to be shook up. He shook his head in silence, then he added, "Just forget that you ever saw that OK my friend?"

"OK Marty. My lips are sealed."... Answered Jeffery as obediently as possible.

Martin knew better, and he wondered if he could trust Jeffery? Maybe Jeffery was gonna have to experience the basement over at the Murder Hotel?

He actually had become friends with Jeffery, and he wanted to push that thought of the basement, right out of his head. In his mind he said... 'No. No. Jeffery is my friend. He won't say anything.'

And he headed down the street to the Hotel.

Not Good News

"YOU DID WHAT?" ...Holmes was extremely upset.

There was a long silence before he spoke up again, *"Goddammit Martin. I told you that something like this might fucking happen. This could turn out to be a real screw up on your part!"*

Martin shook his head, "Look I'm sorry, I will get rid of all the pictures TONIGHT!"

Holmes only stared at the wall. But he said nothing.

That level of silence started to scare Martin, and he wondered if Holmes would do him in over this faux paux.

"Look... I fucked up OK?" ...He paused.

Then he continued, "The owner of the store is a friend, and he's already told me that he'll keep that photo to himself. The only piece of good news is that the woman... I think her name was Edna or something like that, anyway she just looks like she's sitting in that chair naked; with her eyes closed, sucking my dick. I mean, Jeffery never asked anything about whether she was dead or alive. He only saw the picture for a few seconds. I think he was more interested in seeing a naked woman. But yes. I will get rid of **ALL** the pictures tonight."

Holmes was shaking his head in disgust. Then he pointed at Martins ass. And Matin tried to assure him that he would toss the picture in his wallet into the oven along with all the other pictures on the walls downstairs... all the photos, the evidence, would burn up in the oven with no one the wiser.

Holmes remained silent, but he did offer a reassuring nod that everything was alright. It wasn't.

At that precise moment the bell sounded at the front Registration Desk. Holmes made his way to the lobby to see who was there, but along the way he thought to himself, 'You fucken dip ship. That was the last straw.'

Meanwhile Martin felt that he had put up a decent defense regarding his fuck up, and he began to relax a little, he thought to himself... 'Phew, I have to be more careful if I don't want to end up in the goddamn oven downstairs, myself.'

Nowhere to hide

On the premise that he was downstairs to actually check to see that everything that could incriminate the two men was removed, Holmes did a cursory inspection of what Martin had done with all the incriminating photos.

Afterwards he offered a weak smile of approval to Martin, once Martin became comfortable, he turned away to point out something he had done correctly attempting to garner Holmes's approval... , but the moment he turned away... Holms stabbed him in the back of the neck severing his spine, and he fell to the ground grimacing. *"Goddam you fucking prick, what are you doing?"* ...he shouted.

Holmes just stood by while he lay on the floor bleeding to death, *"You've become a liability Martin, sorry my friend, but I cannot tolerate any future risks!"* Moments later Martin was nothing more than a silent ball of flesh on the floor.

Almost immediately Holmes began the process of dismembering the body and stuffing Martin into the open oven.

Once Martin's body was tucked away, he fired up the gas and latched the oven door.

Holmes spent the next hour cleaning up all the blood in an attempt to get the white floor tile, and the wall tile back to its original white luster.

Within two hours Martin was history.

Holmes made his way back upstairs as casually as if he had just come home from a 'day at the office'. It was already late and he had already closed up for the evening, so he focused on trying to get a good night's sleep.

five additional years.

Surprisingly, even after the Expo shut down young attractive women continued to arrive seeking work in Chicago.

But, new faces began to be fewer and fewer. Despite that, every couple of weeks some new victim would show up wanting to rent a room. The pace of the murders had slowed down, and even Holmes started to lose a little interest in maintaining his murderous spree.

Then that same week, a policeman visited Jeffery, the owner of the little grocery store down the street. The same store that Martin would occasionally stop in to purchase liquor. "Hi, my name is Detective Christopher Winslow, I'm with the Chicago Police Department. This is my partner Paul Mathis. Have you got a minute to chat?" and he flashed Jeffery his badge.

"Oh shit, now what?" ...Jeffery asked.

The detective smiled and tried to calm Jeffery down. "No. No. We'd just like to ask you a few questions. We're attempting to locate a fellow by the name of Martin Waxmeir. We were told by his employer that he lived down the street at that corner hotel."

Jeffery rolled his eyes and then said, *"Oh yeah, Martin yeah he used to come in about once a week for a bottle of hootch. I never knew his last name, but he was a weird one."*

The detective in charge glanced at his partner before asking, *"Weird? Like how."*

Hold on one second, and Jeffrey rang up a local woman who had a bottle of milk and a cube of butter. *"That'll be 85¢ Mr. Botticelli, plus 3¢ deposit on the bottle."* With that, the woman reached down into a paper shopping bag and she set an empty milk bottle on the counter.

Jeffery spoke up, *"OK. 85¢ Mrs. Johansen."*

Mrs. Botticelli carefully withdrew some specific coins from a small leather coin purse, paid her bill, and left the store.

Once Jeffery seemed to regain his composure, detective Winslow asked, *"How was he weird? Can you elaborate?"*

"I don't know... He was just sort of OFF if you know what I mean?" ...Jeffery explained.

Then he continued, *"One day he waltzed in here and instead of using a basket like everyone else does, he made repeated trips back-and-forth to the counter just stacking everything up, loosely. You know? Hell, he even tossed his billfold on the counter, and I remember picking it up as he turned. I tried to get his attention as he was walking away, but he flagged me off with his hand and gestured that my store was empty of other customers, so I guessed that he wasn't too worried. As I sat his wallet back down onto the counter it flopped open and that's when I saw a photograph of a naked woman in a chair."* And... Jeffery stopped talking.

"Like a picture of some statue in a museum?" Detective Winslow asked.

"No. No. It was a real woman alright, I recognized her. She used to come into the store as well. She

was sitting in a chair, almost as if she was asleep. Motionless, you know? Almost like she was dead? And Martin was also naked. He was posing with her with a huge smile on his face." ...Jeffery explained.

The detective smiled and shared his response with his partner, then he said, *"Yeah I guess that WOULD be a little bit weird."*

"No. No. The weirdest thing was that Martin had his eh, his..." ...Jeffery hesitated.

The two cops were anxious to hear the rest of his story. *"His what?"*

"He had his penis in her mouth. She was sucking his cock, eh... his penis." ...Jeffery explained.

Detective Mathis was shocked beyond words and he stepped forward as he volunteered, *"No shit! You actually saw his eh, penis in her mouth?"*

Jeffery just nodded, and then Winslow stepped closer to the counter before saying, *"Yeah, that would be a little bit weird. I'm guessing that photos like that are probably illegal as well. This Martin fellow probably wasn't too pleased that you saw that right?"*

Jeffery stood erect as if to demonstrate his feelings about such things and said, *"I should think so!"*

Then he seemed to relax a bit and sat back down on his stool., before resuming his story. *"Then he told me... because we were acquaintances... that he hoped that I would never tell anyone what I had seen. So essentially, until now... I never said a word."*

"Was there any name provided of that woman?" ...The main detective asked.

Jeffery tried to explain, *"No, at least not by that Martin fellow, but that woman use to come in the store. She was a regular... And a real looker, maybe 22 or 23. I mean she was easy on the eyes if you know what I mean. I tried to get chummy with her on a few occasions but no such luck, and then one day she was nice enough to tell me that her name was Carol. Carol Boxliner. I mean with an odd name like that, it's something that you don't soon forget. So, you can imagine what I was thinking when I saw her sucking that guy's prick. It was weird, and it sort of pissed me off too."*

"You must have felt a little jealousy huh?" ...Mathis asked.

"Well, eh, yeah a little. I mean that fucking weirdo? He was a skinny assed freak as far as I was concerned, and even though I had the hots for that Carol woman, I was amazed that a good lookin' gal like her would go after a freak like that Martin character. So, you can imagine my response when I saw her sucking his cock? Yeah, did it bothered me? Yeah I was pissed off. But shit. Life goes on. I mean if she was fucking a guy like that, I'm glad she never gave me the time of day." ...Jeffery tried to reason.

Mathis spoke right up, *"You didn't kill both of them , did ya Jeffery?"*

Jeffery had been rubbing his chin when the assistant asked that question, he dropped his hand to the counter top and gave a very condescending look at the second detective but said nothing.

Detective Winslow chimed in, *"My partner here is a little bit too anxious to solve this case, you'll have to forgive him."*

And the first detective put his hand on his partner's chest and gently nudged him back and away from the counter a few inches, while putting a finger to his own pursed lips. Indicating that he should keep quiet.

He obviously wanted his partner to stay out of this, and that HE would be conducting the investigation.

Then he said, *"No one is prepared to say that we're dealing with a murder here. So far, this Martin fellow and I guess this woman, the woman that you say is known as Carol, are both just missing persons. However, I was wondering if you wouldn't mind helping our investigation by maybe coming down to the police department and working with an artist that we will provide. He can listen to your description of this Martin guy as well as that Carol woman and he can possibly come up with a reasonable sketch of the two of them. That might help us find these people?"*

"Look I'm usually open six days a week, at least until eight or nine PM. I can't afford to hire anyone so I'm literally a captive audience. Actually, I have a small apartment upstairs (and he pointed towards the ceiling). Even if I wanted to kill that prick and his girlfriend, I don't have time to even scratch my own ass. How would I pull that off?" ...and Jeffery stood there with both palms up and his arms outstretched

like the wings of a war plane. Then he added, *"If you want to have an artist work with me, fine! But he'll have to come here. I ain't got time to be gallivanting all over Chicago while some guy draws pictures."*

Detective Winslow began to nod, he was fairly sure that number one... this was still a 'missing persons' case, and <u>not a murder</u>, and number two... this guy was way too busy trying to earn a living in his little grocery store to commit two murders.

But he realized one thing for sure. The parents of a missing woman, who had filed a missing person's report a long, long, time ago... had come all the way to Chicago looking for their daughter. They didn't find her, but Winslow recalled that woman's name was Carol Boxliner.

The two cops excused themselves, and they reconvened back on the sidewalk out of hearing range.

Winslow smacked his partner on the arm. *"What the fuck is wrong with you, asking that guy if he killed those two people?"* Mathis said nothing, and only shrugged his shoulders. Then Winslow added, *"Come on. We need to get back to the precinct."*

The heat is on

Both Detective Winslow and Detective Mathis's patience was beginning to fray.

They had slammed the bell at the registration desk several times with absolutely no response. Finally, Holmes emerged from the back area, *"I'm sorry to keep you waiting gentlemen."* He smiled, *"How can I be of service?"*

Detective Winslow flashed his badge, *"Hello. I'm Detective Winslow and this is detective Mathis."* ...and he held out his free hand to shake.

Holmes just stood there smiling. He did not shake hands. Then he said, *"Holmes. I own this place. How can I help you?"*

"We were wondering if you remember a young woman by the name of Carol Boxliner?" ...Detective Winslow asked.

Holmes scratched his chin and looked off into the void as if thinking. *"Boxliner, Boxliner... Oh yeah I remember her. Yes, she stayed here for a while. And not too long after she left, her parents showed up looking for her. Then, maybe a month later the police stopped by. I guess they were looking for her too."*

Windslow sensed that something was just not right. He asked, *"You guess? You weren't sure?"*

Then Holmes stuttered before trying to clarify, *"Well, yeah... I mean yes, they were trying to find her."*

"Well, she's still considered a 'missing person', and we're still trying to find her." ...Winslow explained.

Holmes just nodded and smiled but offered nothing useful.

After a pregnant pause, Winslow asked, *"How about a guy named Martin Waxmeir? What can you tell us about him?"*

"Well. He worked for me for quite a while. Sort of like a handyman, you know? I felt sorry for him and gave him a part-time position to help him out, you know?" ...Holmes tried to explain.

"I guess you were already aware that he had a full time job down the street at the printing shop, right?" ...Winslow explained.

"Oh Yeah, he only worked here part-time and in return I gave him a place to stay. We essentially traded his labor for the rent. I think, because he was a single fellow, his interest was in meeting a nice woman, and there have been numerous beautiful young women who have stayed here from time to time. I think that's what attracted him to the place?" ...Holmes tried to explain.

Winslow asked, *"Would you mind if we had a chat with Mr. Waxmeir?"*

"No. I wouldn't mind at all, but... I don't know where he is. Recently he stopped showing up. He just disappeared. I waited for more than a week, then I moved all of his possessions to storage and re-rented his room." ..Holmes explained.

"Hummmm. What about his possessions, can we take a look at his things?" ...Detective Winslow asked.

"I'd love to be able to help you fellows out, but it's been at least a few weeks since I got rid of all his junk. I can assure you that it was all just junk. Nothing of value, or I would have just kept it for his back rent."

"I thought that you said you two traded... ***His labor*** *for* ***His rent****. Isn't that what you said."* Detective Winslow pressed Holmes.

Holmes was obviously caught in a lie. He tried to smile as he waved his hand in the air, *"Yeah. I guess... I guess... I forgot. You know I've had several so-called handymen over the years, I must have gotten confused. That's all."*

Windslow smiled, and stood up, *"Well, Thanks for you assistance Mr. Holmes. Here's my business card. If you think of anything that might help us find these two, please get in touch with me."* Holmes took the card and then looked up smiling as he nodded.

Winslow and Mathis left the building. Outside Mathis asked Winslow, *"What do you think?"* Winslow had a scowl on his face when he answered, *"Something is rotten in Denmark."*

Back At the Precent

That afternoon Winslow had an impromptu meeting in Captain Bischoff's office.

As he approached the Captain's office the Captain spotted him and flagged him inside. Winslow took a seat.

"So, what's up?" Captain Bischoff asked.

Winslow tossed a manilla folder onto the Captain's desk, and as the Captain was picking it up, Winslow tried to jiggle his memory. *"You recall that missing person's case, a young woman by the name of Carol Boxliner? Remember, her parents came to Chicago looking for their missing daughter?"*

The Captain suddenly recalled the case, *"Yeah, yeah, that case went cold. So, what's up?"*

"Well. Mathis and me think we may have a new lead." ...Winslow explained.

"OK. I'm listening." ...The Captain answered.

"Well. There's a guy who owns that three story building at the corner of Wallace and 63rd Street? I think he's some kind of physician or something. Anyway, Carol Boxliner rented a room at some point in the past from him."

"OK. But there's nothing illegal about that!" ...The Captain announced.

Winslow chuckled, "That's right, but guess who also lived there?"

The Captain shrugged his shoulders.

"Martin Waxmeir? He was recently reported by his employer as 'missing in action'." ... Winslow explained.

"So? A guy decides to quit his job and leave Chicago, happens every day. What of it?" ...The Captain asked.

"Well, this Martin fellow, as it turns out... may have been having an affair with that Boxliner woman. We don't have the photograph but the owner of a small grocery store just down the street from where he was staying, accidentally saw a photograph in that fellow's wallet that showed him and that women together stark naked, and she had his penis in her mouth." ...Winslow explained.

"No shit?" the Captain exclaimed. Then he asked, *"So what're you thinking?"*

"Mathis and me went over there to speak with the owner. His name is H. H. Holmes. And I think he's trying to hide something. I mean we asked him a few questions and he seemed to trip over his own dick trying to answer us. I don't know, but there's something very suspicious about that guy. I just can't put my finger on it." ...Winslow explained.

"What are you suggesting we do?" ...the Captain asked.

"I think that if we can get a search warrant to search the place, we might be able to solve a lot of Chicago's Mysteries." ...Winslow explained.

It didn't take too long for the Captain to agree, *"OK. But if you come up empty, it will be impossible to get a second search warrant if we decided that it's necessary. The lawyers will have a field day with that one. So, you had better make it count!"* ...The Captain explained.

The search

It took three weeks to secure the search warrant and then when the paperwork came through, Winslow had to jump through additional hoops to pull together a small team of six officers... in addition to his partner Mathis for a total of eight policemen.

A mugshot of serial killer H. H. Holmes from 1895.

Early on a Friday morning the team knocked on the Inn's front door. A few minutes later a sleepy Holmes answered the door. *"Jesus Christ, what in the hell is this all about?"*

Winslow stepped forward and handed the document to Holmes, "It's a legal search warrant! Step aside and read it." And he flagged all of the other officers, who then entered the building.

Holmes protested as loudly as he could until the police found there way down into the basement. That's when he decided that the jig was up. He sat down on a chair and shook his head in disbelief. That's when he surprised the officers by revealing what he had done.

"Well. I've had a good run all of these years. I literally got away with murder. Murders, I should say." ...Holmes revealed.

Winslow asked, *"Exactly how many people have you killed Mr. Holmes?"*

Holmes looked up at Winslow and smiled, *"In Chicago, or in total?"*

"OK. Let's start with Chicago?" ...Winslow asked.

"I'd have to guess, but more than 50." ...Holmes smiled demonically as if proud of his murderous accomplishments. He paused as if to tantalize the cops with his story. Then he added. "Then there were the murders in London."

"You did this in London too?" ...Winslow asked.

"Oh yeah. I was successful there too! They called me 'Jack-the-Ripper' in London" ...Holmes explained.

"Why didn't you just stay there if you were so cunning?" ...Winslow asked.

"Eh, when things heated up, I decided to come to America instead." And then he laughed demonically, "I guess America was just lucky to have me."

There was a long pause and then he held out his arms and one of the officers cuffed him. Then he added, *"I guess the jug is up, huh?"*

"JIG. Yeah the jig is up." ...Winslow corrected him.

November 17, 1894 - The trial

The trial was escalated by the police department.

They wanted the general public to read in the newspapers that important crimes, such as the gruesome crimes that Holmes committed were dealt with promptly.

Without a doubt the Holmes confession was what cinched things up for the prosecution, and he was convicted of capital murder on multiple counts.

Within a few weeks the sentencing part of the trial commenced and Holmes was given the death penalty.

Shortly afterwards Holmes was hung by the neck.

If H. H. Holmes was truly 'Jack-the-Ripper' he may have committed close to seventy-five or more murders over his lifetime. He may have been the worst Serial Killer in history next to William Gacy, and the likes of Ted Bundy.

Normal people will never understand what drives a person to take another human being's life.

But the good news is that eventually justice is carried out.

THE END

About the Author

Denny Magic was born in 1949 in San Francisco, California. He's a retired Hardware/Software Test Engineer, and has worked for many of the big names in the Silicon Valley.

In the early 1980's Denny started writing Stage Plays, Teleplays, Screenplays, and is a published writer of freelance magazine articles. He has written several Children's Story Books (including two with children's author Jeanne Wood, and one with author Kyle Axile). In 2012 he partnered with author Robert Steacy, and together the two wrote what they consider the Final Episode [#6 in the series] of "The Pirates of the Caribbean" franchise.

While working in the engineering field he started his own entertainment production company with partners Randel Chow & Jerry Mahdik, and together they produced several commercial CD projects into the late 1990's, which included two Disney® style musicals, and original Opera, plus one contemporary [easy rock] CD.

In 2006 Denny formed "Denny Magic Studios" which was a California Design Company specializing in Rides, Attractions, and Concessions for Theme Parks, with an emphasis on the Disney® style of 'Dark Rides' (rides that are inside buildings, using animatronic characters, music, and strong storytelling).

The company utilized freelance animators & artists, a conservative number of Creative Writers, and over a dozen gifted music composers from various countries around the world.

www.ingramcontent.com/pod-product-compliance
Lightning Source LLC
LaVergne TN
LVHW040944150826
845672LV00002B/529

9798360928553